Tyla
And The Bully
Ballerina

**Rubie Mizell
and
Tyla'Grace Edgecomb**

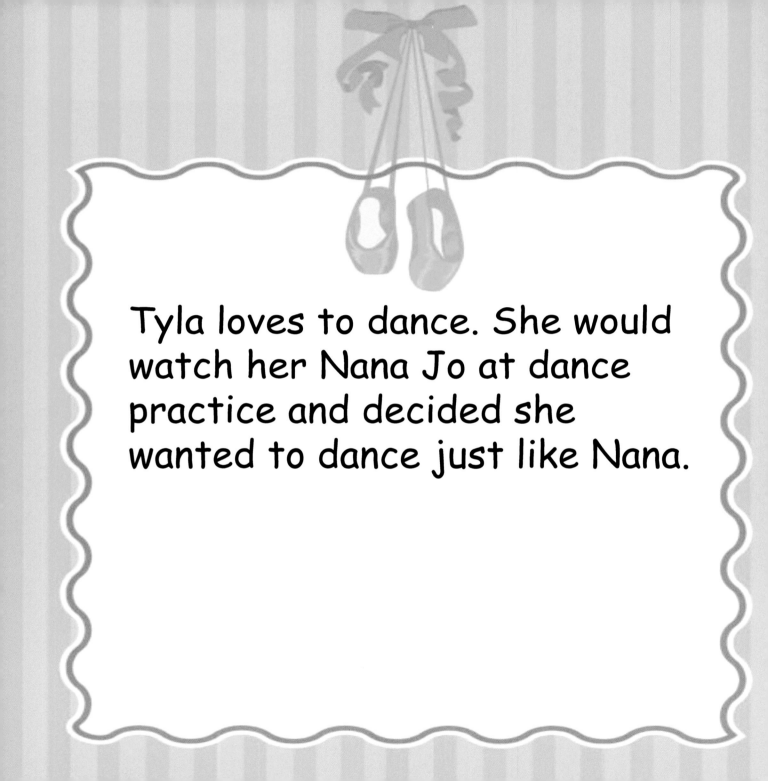

Tyla loves to dance. She would watch her Nana Jo at dance practice and decided she wanted to dance just like Nana.

She is the only girl in her house and has four brothers who love to play sports.

"Yay, it's Saturday!" yelled Tyla. Saturdays were always the best for Tyla, because it was Ballet day. Tyla loves her ballet teacher, Ms. Sonya, and her friends.

Today in class, there was a new girl named Jaz, and she wasn't so nice.

Jaz was teasing everyone in class. Jaz pushed Tyla and laughed when she fell.

"That was not very nice!" said Tyla. Jaz begin to look very sad and said, "I'm Sorry!"
Tyla gave Jaz a hug and said, "I forgive you!"

Jaz was shocked! "But I was mean to you!" Jaz said. "Forgiveness is the entry to the heart." Said Tyla. "God forgives us, so I can forgive you." Tyla learned about forgiveness in Children's Church. Jaz was happy!

Because of Tyla's forgiveness, Jaz was no longer a bully.

Ms. Sonya was so proud of Tyla, that she surprised the class with a pizza party! The children were so happy.

That day all of the children saw the importance of forgiveness.

When Tyla arrived home, she prayed and thanked God for forgiveness.

Bonus: Coloring Sheets

Made in the USA
Middletown, DE
14 December 2019